The Faeries' Promise

Silence and Stone

BY KATHLEEN DUEY

Illustrated by
SANDARA TANG

Aladdin
New York London Toronto Sydney

ALADDIN

An imprint of Simon & Schuster Children's Publishing Division
1230 Avenue of the Americas, New York, NY 10020
First Aladdin hardcover edition July 2010
Text copyright © 2010 by Kathleen Duey
Interior illustrations © 2010 by Sandara Tang
For information about special discounts for bulk purchases, please contact
Simon & Schuster Special Sales at 1-866-506-1949 or business@simonandschuster.com.
The Simon & Schuster Speakers Bureau can bring authors to your live event.
For more information or to book an event contact the Simon & Schuster Speakers
Bureau at 1-866-248-3049 or visit our website at www.simonspeakers.com.
Designed by Lisa Vega
The text of this book was set in Adobe Garamond.
The illustrations for this book were rendered digitally.
Manufactured in the United States of America
0710 FFG
2 4 6 8 10 9 7 5 3
Library of Congress Cataloging-in-Publication Data
Duey, Kathleen.
Silence and stone / by Kathleen Duey ; illustrated by Sandara Tang. — 1st Aladdin hardcover ed.
p. cm. — (The faeries' promise)
Summary: Kidnapped and confined to a room in a castle before she can develop her flying and
magical skills, Alida the faerie patiently plans her escape—with the help of a human boy.
ISBN 978-1-4169-8456-6
[1. Fairies—Fiction. 2. Magic—Fiction.] I. Tang, Sandara, ill. II. Title.
PZ7.D8694Sik 2010
[Fic]—dc22
2009042542
ISBN 978-1-4424-1301-6 (eBook)

With love and thanks to Ellen Krieger,

my editor and friend,

for publishing my first book and so many more

Chapter

1

Alida sat on her blanket, her wings folded.

The bed was far too big for her.

It had been built for a grown-up human to sleep in.

The old man had told her that.

She didn't know his name.

She had no idea why he had lifted her out of her soft faerie's-nest bed and brought her here so long ago.

The wagon wheels had bumped over the rutted road.

They had passed through two towns at night, the last one at the bottom of the hill below the castle. Both had been silent, the windows dark, everyone asleep.

The man had been very careful not to hurt her or scare her on the journey.

He had spoken quietly, kindly, as the horses galloped in the moonlight.

He hadn't told where he was taking her. But he had promised that no one would harm her.

And he had been right—no one had.

Alida remembered seeing the castle guards as the old man led her through the wide halls. But no one had so much as spoken an unkind word. No one had spoken to her at all.

The old man had carried her up the long, twisting stairs into the tower.

He had bent down to kiss her forehead, then he had gone, locking the door behind him. Alida had heard the heavy wooden bar slide into place. It had been dark—she couldn't see how small the chamber was that first night.

She had been frightened, but that had passed. She wished she had asked the old man whose castle this was—which nobleman owned it. But she hadn't thought of it until much later.

Alida missed her family very much. At first she had cried almost every day. But she knew that weeping would not help her make her way home. And so she stopped.

She watched the seasons pass, and she waited.

There was nothing else she could do.

There was a small, barred window near the arched ceiling far above her head. The glass was thick and dirty. But she could see that the sky was deep blue today.

She loved to watch the clouds sail past.

Sometimes she could see the moon.

The chamber was chilly sometimes, but not really cold. It was small, but it was big enough for a faerie. She had grown in the sixty years she had been locked in this chamber, but she was still a child.

Faeries lived much longer than human beings, and they grew much more slowly. But even if she

4

lived to be almost three hundred years old, like her grandfather had, she would never be taller than a seven-year-old human girl.

There was a narrow crack in the stone wall, just wide enough for tiny wisps of wind to sneak in, just wide enough to see out. Peeking through it, Alida had traced the seasons.

Sixty summers had come and gone.

Just as many winters had passed, icy, dark, and deep.

And now spring was near again.

She would be able to see the flowers blooming soon.

Alida slid off the bed and walked to the wall.

She laid her cheek against the cold, gray stone, then turned her head, squishing her nose a little, squinting one eye and closing the other.

It took a little while to find the perfect position, but once she did, she could see through the crack in the stone. There were tall trees, and a narrow road.

Once, she had seen unicorns on that road,

galloping, their heads high, their manes streaming out behind them.

Today there were castle guards walking past, far below the tower.

Their armor was shiny.

Their backs were straight and their tunics were blue and red.

Alida stared past them at the thin slice of woods and meadow—the only part of the world she could see. She could imagine the smell of the dew, the sweet, soft petals of the flowers that would come soon. She smiled. The trees were budding.

Sometimes, if she pressed her ear against the stone, she could hear woodpeckers tapping, hawks calling, and meadowlarks singing.

And if she stood in just the right place, if the day was bright and sunny, if she turned her head perfectly and squinted hard, she could see a little way down the road.

She didn't know where it led. She had no idea

where she would end up if she walked down it. Home?

Oh, how she missed her family. She missed magic. Her older sister would be able to fly well by now. Terra would have been practicing all this time. She would be weaving through the oak forest, higher than the birds, and much more swiftly.

Alida stretched her wings. Any faerie child could rise off the ground. But learning to fly well took a lot of practice. She had just been learning to glide down from the top of the huge egg-shaped rock at the far end of the meadow.

She was sure she wouldn't be able to do even that now.

Alida took one more breath of the cool, sweet air, and then went to sit on the edge of the bed again.

She smoothed her dress. Her mother had made sure that it would grow with her, and that it would stay clean and fresh.

Her mother could work perfect magic of all kinds. So could her father.

Alida often dreamed about the faerie lights flickering in the night. In her dreams she could hear the breathy voices of faerie flutes on the still summer air.

She blinked back sudden tears.

Someday, somehow, she would find her way home.

She climbed back onto the bed and refolded her wings. Then she just sat still and waited for the day to pass.

Chapter

2

The next day Alida woke at sunrise, as always.

And as always, she lay still, her eyes closed, remembering her dreams. This time she had been outside, flying with her sister, looking for lily blossoms. In the dream they were laughing, arguing, racing each other through the trees.

When Alida finally opened her eyes, she saw the gray stone walls. And once again, she had to face the truth. This chamber was real, not her dreams.

She slid out from beneath her blanket and went to peek through the crack in the stone wall. Seeing

the meadow far below soothed her heart, but it made her sad, too.

Standing in the exact center of the little chamber, below the dirty window, she moved her wings as fast as she could.

She stood on the tips of her toes.

But she could not rise into the air now.

Not even a little.

She folded her wings and went to sit on the edge of her bed to wait for the footsteps.

Every day, in the middle of the afternoon, someone brought her food.

There was a slot in the thick ironclad door.

Beneath the slot was a shelf.

Every day someone removed the empty tray from the day before and pushed another one through the slot.

Every day, careful not to touch the iron cladding on the door, Alida slid the tray off the shelf.

Then she sat on her bed to eat.

Alida always ate everything on the tray, because she was hungry. But the food was awful.

It was terrible.

Coarse bread and thin soup, clumped oatmeal and meat.

Human food.

When she was finished, she pushed the tray back through the slot as far as she could.

There was a hinged iron cover over the slot.

It swung both ways.

Alida had tried to see through it a thousand times.

It was impossible.

It swung closed too quickly.

Iron was poisonous to faeries, so she had to be very careful. She had no stick, no broom handle; there was nothing in the chamber that would let her lift the iron cover without touching it. She could not see the humans who brought the trays. But she could hear them.

Some of the tray carriers had been slow, their feet dragging a little as they walked.

Others had louder, faster footsteps.

But they were always heavy footfalls, clomping on the stone floor—always human. Sometimes she heard the tray carrier breathing hard. The stairs that spiraled up the stone tower were long and steep.

At first she had said hello, very quietly.

Then, for a whole year, she had said it louder and louder.

No one had answered her whispers. No one answered her shouts.

She had tried being polite. She said, "Good day!" or "How are you?" but it didn't help. No one ever said anything back.

For a long time, it had made her angry.

Now it only made her sad.

She was lonely. And there was nothing she could do about it. Once there had been a spiderweb on the window above her head. She had loved watching the spider weave its silk. But it was gone. And another one had never come.

Alida stood up and went back to the crack in the stone wall.

She breathed in the smell of sun and wind and rain.

She listened for birdsong and the quick tapping of woodpeckers.

Then she sat on her bed again.

When the footsteps finally came, Alida turned to stare at the locked door. For the first time since she had been here, the footsteps weren't clomping on the stone floor. They weren't heavy.

They were light, graceful.

Not as graceful as a faerie, but almost.

A human *child*?

Alida held her breath.

The footsteps stopped just outside the door, as always.

She watched the empty tray disappear through the slot. Then the iron cover swung back as a new tray slid through.

What happened next astonished Alida. There were no footsteps. There was silence.

Instead of leaving, the food bringer was still standing on the other side of the door.

Alida could hear breathing.

The food bringers had never waited, not even an instant. They always pushed the tray through, then clomped right back downstairs.

"Hello?" she whispered.

There was no answer.

She listened as hard as she could, hoping for a voice, a word or two.

It was silent for so long that she was sure the tray bearer had tiptoed away. But then she heard footsteps, light, graceful footsteps moving away from the door. The sound faded, getting quieter and quieter as the tray carrier went back down the steep stairs.

Alida listened until every tiny sound was gone, her heart beating hard.

She stood on the tips of her toes to reach the tray.

When she pulled it down, she blinked, amazed. There, next to the dark, coarse bread and mushy gray barley soup, was a little bouquet of yellow flowers.

They were shaped like tiny trumpets.

Real food! Faerie food!

She set the tray on her bed, her mouth watering.

Trembling, she ate each flower carefully, slowly, lost in the sweet taste, the wonderful, complicated smell of the petals. And when the flowers were all gone, she twirled in a circle, smiling.

The next day there were more yellow flowers.

They were sweet and fresh. One had a few dewdrops trapped inside.

Alida drank them instantly, using the flower as a tiny cup. She had not tasted dew or rainwater in all the long years she had been locked in this chamber.

She ate the rest of the flowers with her eyes closed, her heart joyful. When she was finished, she danced in circles, twirling and twirling.

Happiness, even just a little happiness, was amazing. The sunlight coming in through the high, dirty window seemed brighter.

The next day there were more flowers on the tray.

This time there were deep red petals mixed in.

Roses? Roses!

"Thank you," she murmured. There was no answer.

She ate the real food and left the bread untouched.

The next day, when she heard the quiet footsteps, she leapt up and stood near the door. "Thank you for the flowers," she said, a little louder than she had before.

There was a long silence. Then the old tray was pulled through the slot and she heard a faint whisper. Too faint.

"I can't hear you," she answered.

She heard the human child take a long breath. "You don't want the bread?"

"Do you want it? The flowers are enough for me," Alida whispered back.

"Yes," came the answer.

The new tray slid toward her. There was a little pile of rose petals, a mound of the yellow flowers, and two fat white lilies.

"Do you like lilies?" It was barely a whisper and she lowered her voice to match it.

"I *love* them."

Alida listened to the footsteps as the tray bearer left, walking light and fast.

Then she ate. And when she was finished, she could hear faerie flutes inside herself. They were playing a tune she had not remembered in a long time. She danced again.

Chapter

3

The next day, Alida's tray had only flowers on it. Lilies and roses.

She listened for the fading footsteps, but there was only silence. She leaned a little closer to the ironclad door. "Are you still here?"

"Yes."

"I haven't talked to anyone for a very long time," she said. When the tray bearer didn't answer, she bit her lip. "What's your name?" she whispered.

There was no answer for so long that she was sure the tray bearer had tiptoed away this time. Then she heard a careful whisper.

"I am called Gavin."

"I am Alida," she whispered back.

"Tell me true," Gavin said. "Are you a faerie?"

"Yes."

She heard him take a quick breath. "You are? Faeries are *real*?"

"What a foolish thing to ask!" Alida snapped, startled by the insult.

Gavin didn't answer. She stared at the high window and waited, hoping he would at least say good-bye.

He didn't. He just walked away.

Why would he answer?

Alida was furious with herself for being so rude.

She had talked to only a few humans in her life. Maybe he had never seen a faerie. If he had always lived in towns, or in this castle, it was possible. Faeries lived in the woods.

She walked in circles, then sat on her bed, scared.

What if Gavin stopped bringing her flowers? What if he never spoke to her again?

The next morning she woke even earlier than usual.

To keep from worrying about how angry Gavin was, she danced a little, singing a song her mother had taught her. The words were odd, and she wasn't sure what they meant. But singing it made her feel better.

Then she went to look outside. Squinting to see through the crack, she stared at the yellow blooms beneath the trees.

A sudden motion caught her eye.

Someone was moving along the edge of the woods.

It was a human, a boy, picking flowers.

Gavin?

He had hair the color of wheat straw. He looked small from the height of the tower. His trousers and shirt looked too loose. He was thin.

Alida watched.

He was slow and careful. He didn't uproot the plants. He held still when he startled a few sparrows, so that he wouldn't scare them any more than he already had.

Alida watched until he had gone too far for her to see. Then she went to sit on the edge of her bed and waited.

She jumped up when she heard footsteps.

As soon as he had pushed the tray through, she stood on her tiptoes to see better. Oh! Lilies, roses, some of the yellow flowers, and a few dark blue pansies!

"Oh my," she breathed. "Thank you!" Then she spoke a little louder. "I am sorry I was rude."

"It's all right," Gavin whispered back. "It must be hard for you to be locked in."

Alida wasn't sure what to say to that, so she didn't even try. "I think I saw you this morning," she told him. She explained about the crack in the wall. "Is your hair the color of wheat straw?"

He didn't answer. Maybe it scared him to know she had watched him.

Some humans were afraid of faeries.

"I would never play a trick on you," she said.

Alida hoped he believed her. It was true. And, really, she *couldn't*. She had learned only one small bit of magic before she had been brought to this place. She could make a flower drop into her hand without touching it.

Or at least she had been able to before she came here. Maybe she couldn't now. She hadn't practiced.

"Whose castle is this?" Alida whispered. "Which nobleman owns it?"

There was a long pause, as if Gavin was wondering if he should answer. Then he finally whispered, "Lord Dunraven."

Alida felt her heart sinking. She remembered her mother crying, telling her that the Dunravens all hated magic and acted like they owned the world.

"Do you know why I am here?" she asked Gavin.

Gavin didn't answer.

Had she upset him again?

24

Even in whispers, even through a door, it was so lovely to talk to *someone*. She was about to apologize when he spoke.

"Can you fly?"

"Not now," she said, and felt an ache of sorrow in her throat.

"But you could? Before you came here?"

"Almost," she told him. "I was learning. I can't now."

"Are your wings broken?"

"No." Alida stiffened her wings and vibrated them.

"Magic is real?" he whispered.

"Of course," she answered, and knew she sounded impatient.

"I will be back tomorrow," he whispered, and she heard his quick, sudden footsteps as he ran back toward the long staircase.

Alida opened and closed her wings.

She had to stop snapping at Gavin. It was not his fault she was here.

The next day he brought her more flowers and stood outside the door while she began to eat.

"Can you work magic?" he whispered.

Alida thought he was about to ask her for a wish. Humans often asked faeries for favors like that.

She started to tell him that she wasn't sure, that she had learned only very small magic from her mother and hadn't practiced it at all. The truth was, she hadn't really even thought about practicing. Why?

"Can you work magic?" Gavin asked again, a little louder.

She took a breath, about to explain, but then he spoke again.

"Can you help someone get well?" he whispered.

Alida stood on her tiptoes, her wings spread.

She was about to admit the truth—but then she thought about it.

Did Gavin know someone who was sick?

Maybe, if he thought she could help, he would open the door. Maybe she *could* go home!

Alida took a long breath. She closed her eyes. Then she lied.

"Yes," she said. "I know how to help someone get well."

Gavin didn't say anything. Alida listened to his footsteps—he was running toward the stairs. She sat on the edge of her bed for a long time, ashamed of the lie, but excited, too.

Would he open the door?

Would he let her out of this chamber?

If he did, they could go find her family together.

Faeries didn't always like being bothered by humans asking for magic. But this would be different. Her family would be very glad to see her safe and sound. And her mother would be happy to help Gavin—to thank him.

Alida knew she couldn't make anyone get well.

But her mother could.

So the lie wouldn't matter.

Chapter

4

Gavin didn't talk to Alida the next day.

Or the next.

Or the one after that.

He brought her trays heaped with flowers, then left without a word.

She whispered hello to him every time, but he didn't answer.

Was he angry?

Had he known she was lying?

Alida ate every petal of every flower. She even chewed up the stems. And every day she felt stronger.

On the fourth morning, when she woke, she smelled rain.

Rain!

She slid out of her blanket and looked up at the barred window high above her head. There were raindrops spattering on the dusty glass.

Alida flexed her wings, pacing, wishing it would storm and wash the window clean. It didn't. There was just a gentle pattering of raindrops.

Alida looked through the crack in the stone and saw Gavin gathering flowers again.

When he finally brought the tray, the flowers were soaked with rain.

"I thought you would like it," he whispered. "But I can dry the petals off if you want me to."

"I am so glad you didn't," she whispered. "I've missed rainwater almost as much as I have missed flowers. And the sky. And talking to someone."

He didn't answer, but she didn't hear him walking away, either.

Alida tried to think of something to more say,

but she was too hungry to think. She nibbled at one of the lilies.

It was delicious.

The drops of rainwater made her sigh.

Eating real faerie food reminded her of her family, her home, of everything she loved. And it made her feel a little stronger every day.

"Thank you," she whispered. "I am so grateful."

She heard the door creak and jumped back. Was he leaning against it?

"If I help you get out of here," he said quietly, "will you help my grandmother get well?" Before she could answer, he went on, "My parents died of the fever when I was a baby. She is the only family I have." She heard him take a long breath, then he said, "Please don't lie to me."

Alida lifted her wings, then folded them tight again.

If she told Gavin the whole truth, she might stay here forever. And she *could* help his grandmother, she would just have to find her mother first.

"Yes," she said, barely breathing the word. Then she forced herself to say it so he could hear it. "Yes! I can help her." Alida held her breath.

"I'll come back tonight just before moonrise," he whispered. "Be ready."

Alida couldn't hear him walking away because she was dancing. She whirled around and around until she was out of breath. Then she walked on her tiptoes, feeling fluttery.

When she finally calmed down enough to look around the chamber, she realized that the only thing she had to carry home with her was her blanket.

She folded it in half, then rolled it up, very carefully. Her mother had woven it for her. It was magical, like her dress; it wasn't faded or dirty.

It weighed less than a hummingbird.

Faeries' looms were strung with spider silk.

The weft threads were spun from thistledown.

Alida sat on the edge of the too-big bed for a

while, then got up and walked along the wall, sliding her fingers along the cool, gray stone.

She had been here so long, it would be very odd to leave.

Her mother would be so happy to see her.

Her sister would dance and sing.

Her whole family—and everyone else—would celebrate.

Alida imagined the feast.

Her family would let Gavin stay because he had saved her.

He might be too big to sit at the table.

Maybe she could sit beside him on the grass.

She closed her eyes and imagined the faerie lights, drifting in the air, the singing and the laughter. It would be *wonderful* to be back with her family.

Chapter

5

lida refused to lie down. She sat upright, listening, scared Gavin would come and she wouldn't hear him.

When she finally did hear his footsteps, she was so excited she jumped off the bed, fluttering her wings. She glided for an instant before her feet touched the stone floor.

"Are you ready?" Gavin whispered.

"Yes!" she whispered back.

She heard a soft, grating sound.

Gavin was sliding the heavy wooden bar that held the door shut.

She stood very still, hoping he was strong enough not to drop it.

A loud noise might bring a guard to come and look.

She heard a small clunk, no more than that.

The door creaked a little.

And then, suddenly, it swung wide open.

Gavin held a little box lantern in one hand. He raised it high. His eyes were wide and his hair looked even lighter in the candlelight. He was staring at her. No. Not at her—at her *wings*.

"I can't believe it," he whispered. "You *are* real."

Alida had never seen a human boy this close before—but she knew *he* was real.

"Why haven't you ever seen a faerie?" she whispered.

Gavin tilted his head; then she saw his expression change. "You don't know about Dunraven's law, do you?"

She shook her head.

"It's the reason you're here," he whispered. "Sixty years ago Lord Dunraven's great-grandfather forbade faeries to see or speak to humans. It still isn't allowed—not ever, for any reason. It's the same for unicorns and dragons."

Alida was too stunned to say anything.

Gavin lowered the box lantern and gestured for her to come out.

She took the first step, then the second.

She was feeling scared, joyous, grateful to Gavin, and furious with the old Lord Dunraven, all at once. She looked around. The little lantern was bright enough to cast dim light on the walls. The outer room was even bigger than she remembered.

She stared upward at the painted ceiling while Gavin set the heavy wooden bar back into place.

"I brought a shawl for you," he whispered as he turned, untying a length of cloth from around his waist. "To hide your wings."

Alida frowned and clutched her bundled blanket.

35

"You have to," Gavin insisted. "If anyone sees us, they should think we're a brother and sister—farm children."

Alida shook her head. "I can't," she whispered. "It's too heavy, and it will hurt my wings and—"

"No it won't," he interrupted. "Hurry!"

Alida took the shawl from him. It weighed almost nothing. The yarn had been spun from spider silk and thistledown and it was the perfect size. She looked up at him, amazed. "This is faerie cloth," she whispered.

Gavin didn't answer. He pointed at the stairs and led the way.

Alida counted two hundred stairs as they went down, down, down, and out of the tower.

They turned into the first wide, echoing hallway and kept walking, quietly and quickly.

The castle was bigger than Alida could have imagined. It would have been easy to get lost, but Gavin knew the way.

Sometimes Alida could hear faint voices.

Once, in a long corridor, she saw barred doorways, one after another. And behind two of the doors, she heard angry shouts that echoed off the walls. Guards arguing? Or prisoners?

Gavin walked faster, and she had to run to keep up.

The voices faded when they turned a corner into another stone corridor. Gavin stopped suddenly and pulled her into the shadows near the wall.

There were guards ahead of them.

They were carrying torches, their polished armor shining.

None of the guards looked back. Gavin and Alida stood still, barely breathing, until they were out of sight. Then Gavin led Alida up the corridor and around another corner.

She was glad when he finally stopped and pushed open a huge door.

There was nothing but darkness beyond it—and the smell of a forest.

Alida followed him outside.

"See the stables?" he whispered.

She nodded. There was just enough starlight to see the shape of a long, low building. Carriages were lined up along one side.

As they got closer, she smelled hay and the sweet scent of horses' breath. She heard a chicken cluck, soft and sleepy. Then footsteps. Heavy ones.

"Is that you?" It was an old man's voice, and she knew it instantly. He was the one who had brought her here.

She spun around and ran.

Gavin chased her and managed to grab her hand. He pulled her to a stop.

"That's the man who—who—," she stammered.

"I know," Gavin interrupted her. "John brought you here because he had no choice. He will help you now. He'll carry food up the stairs every day so no one realizes you're gone. He's lending us his own mare to ride too, so no one will notice a horse is missing."

"Why?" Alida demanded. "Why would he?" She jerked her hand free. "I can't trust him."

"I'll explain as much as I can later," Gavin interrupted. "We have to leave now." He was watching her closely. She could tell he was ready to grab her again if he had to.

Alida heard the soft clopping of a horse's hooves.

"Get up, boy," the old man said to Gavin as he led a snow-white mare into the moonlight. "I can help the faerie-child."

Alida stared at him, her wings folded tight against her back.

Gavin swung up onto the mare's back.

"I know," John said quietly. "I will be very careful of your wings."

Alida backed away, but the old man was quick. His big, weathered hands swooped her up and set her on the mare before she could react.

There was no saddle.

Alida settled her rolled-up blanket between

herself and Gavin and arranged the shawl.

"Be alert, boy," Old John said. "Care well for her."

"I will," Gavin told him. Then he looked over his shoulder at Alida. "Hang on," he said.

Alida put her hands around his waist.

She had never ridden a horse before.

It felt very strange.

Gavin started off slowly, keeping the mare to a quiet walk, guiding her off the road and into the woods. Alida knew why. He didn't want anyone to hear them leaving, and they had to make their way around the town at the bottom of the hill without being seen.

She looked back at the castle and counted ten towers.

They all had little windows high on the walls.

She had no idea which of them had been hers.

For a long time, they kept to the shadows and let the mare pick her way. Neither of them said a word. Alida was excited, breathless. The forest smelled sweet and clean. It was so wonderful and strange to be outside that for a long time, she kept hoping it wasn't all a dream.

Once they were a good distance from the castle, and long past the little town, Gavin guided the mare back toward the road.

Alida looked through the trees and saw the moon coming up.

It was plump and lovely, the color of hens' eggs.

The mare's hooves made a clopping sound on the hard-packed dirt of the road. "Hold on," Gavin warned her, looking at her over his shoulder again. Then he leaned forward, and the mare rose into a rocking-horse canter.

Alida found her balance and matched the mare's rhythm.

It was scary, but only at first. The sound of the mare's hooves on the road was graceful, musical.

The moon rose higher.

The stars moved across the sky.

The night passed, moment by moment.

When the sun came up, they found a thick stand of trees close to the road.

The mare grazed.

Gavin sat down and leaned against a tree trunk and fell asleep. Alida wrapped herself up in her blanket and stared at the limbs overhead for a long time.

Then she slept too.

They woke up midday and went on.

Alida asked about the law again, and Gavin repeated what he had told her.

"But my family lives in a forest not far from the town of Ash Grove," she said. "We often see humans."

"That's where we're going. But your family isn't there anymore," Gavin said. "The faeries moved far away from people when the law was made."

Alida felt almost dizzy. "How will I find them?"

"I know someone who can probably help you,"

Gavin said, and glanced back at her. "Don't worry."

Alida nodded, but she felt lost and sad. Her home was no longer her home? The big meadow and the huge, smooth rock?

All the sleeping nests high in the trees, all the faerie lights she remembered, the forest . . . Was the meadow near Ash Grove empty?

She wasn't going home, after all.

That afternoon they found a creek and washed their hands and faces. Gavin had a piece of bread in his pocket. Alida found flowers. The mare grazed again while they both napped. Then they went on.

The next day, Gavin kept the mare at an easy jog through the woods. When the sun went down again, he guided her back to the road, so she wouldn't stumble over brambles or fallen limbs in the dark.

"We're more than halfway to Ash Grove," Gavin told Alida.

As the moon rose, he nudged the mare into a canter again.

For a long time, the mare's hoofbeats were the only sound.

Then the rhythm changed—it echoed.

Alida sat straighter, then twisted to look behind them.

"What?" Gavin reined in.

"I thought I heard . . . ," she began, and then stopped. There it was again—faint hoofbeats behind them.

It wasn't one horse, or two.

It was ten or more, coming at a gallop.

Lord Dunraven's guards? It had to be. Farmers did not race down roads in the dark.

"Hold on!" Gavin whispered, and the mare sprang into a gallop. He urged her faster and faster and faster, until they were pounding around a long curve in the road.

Then Gavin reined in hard, and the mare jolted to a stop.

"Hide in the woods, Alida," he said. "Hurry! I'll lead them away."

"We can both hide and—," Alida began, but he slid off, lifting her down before she could say more.

"No. I brought this." He pulled a gold bracelet out of his pocket. "So if they catch up with me, they will think I am a simple thief. They still won't know you are gone."

He bent his knees to look into her face. "If I don't come back, follow this road to Ash Grove. Find Ruth Oakes; you can trust her. Help my grandmother. And don't let *anyone* see your wings."

Gavin jumped back on the mare. "Hide!" he hissed. "Run!" And then he was gone, the mare leaping back into her swift, long stride.

Alida sprinted into the trees.

She crouched, shaking, listening to the hoofbeats getting louder. The horses thundered around the long curve and passed Alida. She shivered in the dark and saw the faint shine of their armor. And then they were gone.

The hoofbeats dimmed.

The forest was suddenly deep and dark and silent.

The stars were ice-silver overhead.

And Alida was alone.

She began to walk, shivering, the shawl tight around her shoulders.

Chapter

6

Alida walked in the darkness beneath the trees that grew alongside the road.

With every step, she hoped Gavin had been able to hide. Maybe he was just waiting for her to catch up to him.

Any moment now, he would whisper her name.

They would hide together and wait for the guards to ride past again, on their way back to Lord Dunraven's castle.

But he didn't whisper.

The road was empty, the forest silent.

Without Gavin, without the mare's hoofbeats, the silence crowded close to Alida.

She could hear her own thoughts.

John had been *old* sixty years before when he had taken her to the castle and carried her up the long, steep stairs.

Humans didn't live that long.

It was magic of some kind.

Was John's long life a gift from a faerie? Or a unicorn, or a dragon? It had to be.

Alida shivered.

Why had her mother let John take her away?

And why hadn't her mother ever come to make sure she was all right?

Alida pulled the shawl closer.

An owl hooted, soft and sleepy.

She walked a little faster.

She wanted to get back to her family, and she wanted Gavin to be all right.

Maybe he was, she told herself as she walked.

Maybe she would catch up, find him hiding in the woods waiting for her.

But she didn't.

By the time the sun came up, she was weary, but she didn't stop.

Then, just after dawn, she heard hoofbeats ahead of her.

Alida ducked behind a tree, peeking out.

The sound got louder and louder.

It was Lord Dunraven's guards, riding back toward the castle. She could see Gavin among them. His hands were tied. A guard held the reins, leading the white mare.

Alida's heart ached as they passed.

Her wings vibrated beneath the shawl.

If she could keep up with them, when the guards stopped to rest, or sleep, she might have a chance to free Gavin before they got him to the castle.

Once they were out of sight, she pulled the shawl off and spread her wings.

She tried to fly.

She tried *so* hard.

She could move her wings so fast they made a whirring sound. But when she stood on her toes and tried to lift herself up into the air, she still couldn't.

She tried again and again.

Her eyes filled with tears. She couldn't do it. She couldn't help Gavin.

Would John? He might.

And Alida was sure her mother would, once she found her family.

Cold, worrying, Alida started walking again. She had to find Ruth Oakes, then her mother, and somehow she would help Gavin.

She kept walking and found wildflowers—lobelia and mallow. She ate as many as she could hold, then kept going.

That morning she saw a few farm wagons on the road and hid as they passed. By afternoon, there were many more.

Most were stacked with early potatoes and bags of last year's barley.

Some had spring onions and radishes.

Human food.

Where were they taking it? Ash Grove? She remembered a market there.

Alida rerolled her blanket, tied her shawl tightly, and made her way to the edge of the road. She stood up straight as a wagon approached her.

"I beg your pardon," she called out.

The driver was an older woman. She looked weary. She didn't answer.

"Pardon me!" Alida shouted again.

The woman just shook her head as the wagon rolled past.

The next farmer pretended not to see her at all.

Alida wondered if they could tell she was a faerie and were afraid to talk to her.

But they didn't look afraid. They looked tired and grumpy.

The wagon after that was pulled by a team of oxen, and the driver raised his eyebrows when Alida spoke.

"Is Ash Grove much farther?" Alida shouted.

He shook his head.

"Is that where you are all taking the food?"

He looked at her as though she had said something puzzling. Then he said, "It's market day tomorrow," in the tone of voice someone would say, "The sky is blue."

Alida watched as he passed. His wagon was only half full of green squash.

She thought he might offer to let her ride.

But he didn't. He cracked his whip, and the oxen flicked their ears.

Alida watched a few more wagons go by.

Then the road was empty for a while.

Alida walked a little faster, thinking. She never wanted to eat human food again. If there weren't wildflowers around Ruth Oakes's house, she would have to find woods where she could gather what she needed.

"Look out!" someone shouted.

Alida jerked around to see a cart coming close.

She jumped backward and felt her shawl slip as she caught her balance.

She dropped her blanket to free her hands, then pulled the shawl back into place.

The cart driver whipped his horses into a trot and disappeared around a curve in the road.

Alida was scared.

Had he seen her wings? Would he tell the guards if they came looking for her?

Alida picked up her blanket and walked back into the woods.

She stayed hidden as long as she could, but then the road crossed a planked bridge.

It was narrow and long.

The river below it was deep blue and swift.

If she could have flown, she would have found a hidden place and been across in a few heartbeats.

But she couldn't.

She had no choice.

She had to climb back up on the road and walk alongside the carts.

They got closer and closer as the road narrowed.

The drivers looked impatient.

Alida kept her eyes down and clamped her blanket beneath one arm so she could hold her shawl in place.

She was nervous.

She kept her wings folded tightly and wondered how old she looked to the humans around her.

John had called her a faerie child.

She was!

But she was probably twice as old as most of the cart drivers.

The wagons came to a stop in the middle of the bridge. Alida heard a few shouts on the far side. Someone was yelling for help.

Alida lowered her head, weaving her way through cart wheels and horses until she was across the river. As she stepped off the bridge, she saw the problem:

A woman's wagon wheel had broken. Five or six men were working to fix it.

Once Alida was across, she veered into the woods again, without glancing back.

She tried to look like she knew where she was going.

She didn't.

But she found a place to hide.

She waited until the overloaded cart blocking the way was moved.

Then she waited until all the cart drivers who had seen her were long gone.

Only then did she come back to the road.

This time she waited until she saw a human girl, walking alone. "Excuse me? Do you know Ruth Oakes?" she asked.

The girl turned to look at her. "Are you sick?"

Alida shook her head, wondering if she looked pale. Probably. She was scared.

The girl pointed. "Go that way until you get to

River Road. Then turn right and walk past all the old farms until you see a neat cottage on the right-hand side. It has rose gardens and flowers."

Alida thanked her and walked away before the girl could ask her anything more. The road was crowded with carts and wagons until she got past Market Square. After that, it was empty.

At the edge of town, Alida heard meadowlarks calling.

Her fear eased.

The crossroads were easy to find.

So was the pretty cottage out on River Road.

Alida stopped in front of it and looked up at the sky. It was so wonderful to be outside, far away from Lord Dunraven's castle.

Without Gavin's help, she would still be peeking through the tiny crack in the stone. She wanted to help him and his grandmother.

And if she could, she would.

Chapter

7

Alida knocked softly the first time.

No one called out. No one came to the door.

She knocked again. Then she stepped back, waiting, holding her breath until she had to let it out.

Alida walked up to the door again, and this time she knocked as hard as she could—but it made no difference.

No one came.

Maybe Ruth Oakes was in Market Square, buying food with everyone else in Ash Grove.

Alida sat on the porch for a while.

Then she walked around the cottage.

The backyard was as neat and pretty as the front yard. There was a beautiful garden, full of flowers. Beyond it were a tidy barn, a wagon shed, and what looked like a doghouse.

That made Alida uneasy—faeries were not usually fond of dogs.

Dogs ran through the forest barking.

They scared the deer and the birds. And they trampled flowers.

Grown-up faeries tricked dogs.

She had seen her mother magically lift a startled dog—moving it back a long way, then letting it sink gently to the ground.

It had run off, barking.

Alida remembered her father lifting heavy field stones without touching them too.

But she didn't know how to work magic yet, so she just stood still, watching the little door of the doghouse, ready to run since she couldn't fly.

But no dog came out of the little house.

Once she was sure she was alone, Alida wandered through the garden.

There were wood's herbs planted everywhere. Meadow flowers had been mixed with roses and tall purple irises.

Alida stared at the roses.

There were a hundred blooms, at least.

She couldn't see anyone, but she wanted to make sure.

"Hello?" she said, raising her voice. "Ruth Oakes? Are you here? Is anyone here?"

There was no answer.

Alida glanced at the house, the barn, and the doghouse. Then she plucked a single rose.

She ate it as fast as she could. When there was still no sound from inside, she picked another bloom and ate it, too.

Then a third.

And a fourth.

She tried to make the fifth one drop into her hand without touching it.

She couldn't.

But maybe she would be able to learn magic soon.

By the barn, she found a rain barrel. She dipped up rainwater in her hands and drank as much as she could hold.

Then she walked back to the front porch.

There was nothing left to do but wait.

She sat down on the steps, facing the road.

The sun was going down by the time Alida finally heard the squeaking of wooden wagon wheels.

She hid, watching.

A sleek bay horse pulled the wagon around the corner and down the path that led to the barn behind the house.

Alida could hear women's voices, then a dog barking, then silence. She waited, scared, hoping the dog wouldn't come running back around the house on its own.

It didn't.

And when she heard two women laughing, her fear eased.

Their voices got a little louder, then Alida heard the sound of the back door opening and closing.

She waited.

Before long she saw lantern light coming from the windows. Then she gathered her courage and knocked on the door.

The voices stilled.

There was a silence, then a sliding sound, and the door opened a little. "Who is there?"

"My name is Alida," she said, standing in the shadows.

"I am Ruth Oakes," the woman said, leaning out, squinting. "Are you ill? Are you in need of my help?"

"No," Alida said, and finally understood why the

girl in Ash Grove had thought she might be sick. Ruth Oakes was a healer.

"Are you by yourself, child?"

It was a different voice. Someone she couldn't see.

"Yes," Alida answered.

Ruth smiled. "Come in." She opened the door wider. "Are you hungry?"

Alida pulled her shawl closer and picked up her blanket, hugging it against her chest. Then she went up the steps. Ruth stood back to let her in.

The cottage was neat and clean. It smelled of herbs, bread, and meat stew. Human food.

"This is my friend Molly Hamilton," Ruth said.

Alida nodded, smiling nervously at the woman who stood by the hearth, stirring whatever was in a big black pot.

"Please join us for supper," Molly said, standing up. Her hair was white, but her back was straight, and she walked with a quick, firm step. So did Ruth. Their cheeks were rosy from the night air.

"A boy named Gavin told me to come here," Alida said, and both Ruth and Molly turned to look at her.

"Are you the—?" Molly whispered, and stopped.

"Of course she is," Ruth interrupted. "Gavin found her!" She gestured toward a chair.

Alida sat, careful to keep her wings folded tightly against her back beneath the shawl.

"I can't believe it!" Molly said.

Alida took a long breath, but she had no idea what to say.

"Gavin is my grandson," Molly began quietly. "But he is like a son to me. Where is he?"

Alida opened her mouth to speak, but she still couldn't find a place to start. Molly didn't look ill. Had Gavin lied for some reason?

"Tell me. Is he in danger?" Molly asked.

Alida nodded. "I think he might be."

Molly dropped into a chair across from her, waiting, her eyes clouded with worry. Ruth stood against the far wall, silent.

"Start at the beginning," Molly said.

Alida began slowly, then the words poured out. She told them about the little chamber, the endless silence, then Gavin's kindness. She explained their agreement and their escape. Then she told them where Gavin was now.

Molly's eyes shone with tears. "I was terribly sick. But with Ruth's help, and a thousand cups of her foul herb teas, I've gotten over it. We sent word to Gavin. We've been expecting him to come back. We never thought . . ." She lifted one hand and gestured at Alida.

"It's my fault they caught him," Alida explained. "I promised him I would help you get well and let him think I could work magic. I can't, but I knew my mother would help. I didn't know my family was gone." She looked at the two women, who were staring at her. "Do you know where they went? My mother can help Gavin. And she will. He saved my life."

Ruth shook her head, "No one knows where

the faeries went after Old Lord Dunraven made his cruel law."

"I can't fly," Alida said, wanting them both to understand. "Or I would have followed the guards and helped Gavin myself." She explained how he had protected her—how he'd made sure the guards would think he was a common thief. "John will pretend I'm still there," she told them. "Maybe he can help Gavin."

Molly wiped at her tears. Then she looked up. "I know you've done your best. I can see it in your eyes."

But Alida knew her best hadn't been enough.

"We will decide what to do in the morning," Ruth said. "Are you hungry? I have roses."

Alida blushed. "No, thank you. I picked some earlier—before you got home."

The fire was warm, and Alida began to realize how tired she was. Ruth made a pallet on the floor for her, off to the side. "Just sleep now," she said.

"We'll eat, then do the same. Tomorrow will be a long day, and we will all need our strength."

Alida took her shawl off and got settled as the two women went into the kitchen.

They talked in low voices.

She tried to overhear but couldn't, and her eyes finally closed.

Chapter

8

Alida woke to hear Ruth and Molly arguing in whispers.

"There is no reason for you to go," Ruth was saying. "None."

"He is my grandson!"

"I know that!" Ruth said. "And that's why you should stay here, so in case things go wrong, you can help him later. Or simply be here when he makes his way home. I am the one who should go."

"Too many people depend on you here," Molly hissed back at her.

Alida sat up.

In the daylight, she could see into the next room.

The women were sitting at the table, teacups in their hands, glaring at each other.

She slipped from beneath her blanket, then out the front door.

It was a beautiful morning, the sun just coming up.

Alida could smell the roses.

She walked around the side of the house, thinking furiously.

Ruth and Molly were both wrong.

Neither of them should go. Gavin needed his grandmother alive and well, and Ash Grove needed its healer.

And they were both old women.

The castle was huge.

What if they had to run up and down tower stairs?

Whoever went would have to sneak around the castle for a long time to find out where Gavin was. Alida could be quieter than any human.

Alida noticed Ruth's wagon by the barn and stared at it.

Could either of the women ride a horse?

Wagons were slow and clumsy—it would take twice as long to get back to the castle in a farm wagon. And the guards would see them coming.

Alida walked to the rose garden and began to eat, chewing fast. If the guards had galloped all night, rested a little, then gone on, they would be back at the castle by now. Maybe Gavin was locked in one of the towers.

Alida sighed. There was no reason for her to stay here another minute. She was going back to the castle.

Alone.

Gavin had saved her life, and he would—

Her thoughts stopped when she heard a low growl.

Alida whirled around just in time to see Ruth's dog running toward her.

Its teeth were bared, its ears flat against its head.

An instant later she was hovering above the ground, her heart pounding inside her chest.

Alida looked down at the dog. Its muzzle was gray. It was old and panting, but it still jumped up, over and over, trying to reach her.

She felt breathless, scared, and amazed.

She was flying!

The dog gathered itself and jumped at her again, coming closer this time. She flew higher without an instant's thought, and its teeth clacked on thin air.

Alida had no idea what had happened.

Why could she fly? She had tried so hard to follow the guards and hadn't been able to. Was it because she had finally eaten faerie food long enough to get her strength back? Or was it something about being outside the cold stone and back where she could smell trees and see the sky? Maybe she had just been so scared of the dog she hadn't had time to think?

Whatever it was, flying felt wonderful, joyous, *right*.

She went a little higher, then stopped, her wings whirring.

74

The house looked small, and for a moment she was scared again. So she glided a little lower, feeling the strength in her wings. Her fears eased.

Alida heard the back door open—Molly and Ruth were coming outside.

Startled, she whirled midair, flying up and over the roof to the front yard, so the dog wouldn't see her. She came lightly to the ground and stood still.

Her wings felt different.

She felt different.

She could fly. Now all she needed was a lot of practice.

On the other side of the house, Ruth was calling the dog.

Its name was Kip, and it stopped barking when it heard her.

Alida lifted her wings. She stood on her toes and rose into the air.

She found a high limb where she could sit, looking down into the backyard.

Ruth was rubbing Kip's ears and telling him not to bark unless he had a reason.

Alida leaned forward to see better.

She slid off the limb and let herself fall a little ways before she spread her wings.

It was so much fun she got back onto the branch and did it again.

When she hovered the second time, she saw Ruth looking up at her. Molly was facing the other way, looking at the garden. Ruth tapped Molly's shoulder. Then they were both staring upward.

Alida flew down to stand beside them.

"Alida is our friend," Ruth scolded Kip gently. "You need to be polite."

Alida watched Kip's ears droop. He looked sorry, then wagged his tail.

"He has never met a faerie," Ruth said, "though he has known a unicorn or two. He was protecting us."

Alida nodded. She watched Kip wag his tail and let him sniff at her hands.

She started to tell Ruth that she had seen unicorns once, galloping into the woods beyond Dunraven's castle. But there was no time for stories.

She stood straight and looked from Ruth's face to Molly's, then back. "Neither one of you should go to the castle," she said. "I should."

Chapter

9

It took a long time to convince them, even though she could tell they knew she was right.

Once the argument was over, they helped her get ready.

Ruth picked a sack of roses.

Molly handed Alida a corked bottle she had filled from the rain barrel.

"You could ride my horse," Ruth said, at least a dozen times.

Alida kept shaking her head.

She had never felt stronger in her life. She had never wanted to do anything as much as she wanted to help Gavin. She didn't want the guards to hear her galloping up the road. And she was almost certain she could fly faster than a horse could gallop.

"You must remember the law," Molly said as they stood in the front yard together.

"I will," Alida promised. "No one will see me."

Ruth had given her a bag. It held her blanket, the shawl, the roses, and the water bottle. "Good-bye," she said solemnly. "I am forever grateful to you both."

Ruth smiled. "And Kip. He taught you to fly."

Alida opened her eyes wide and made a face like she was scared.

They all laughed, but it was thin and quick. They were all worried about Gavin.

"Take care," Molly said. "Come back to us with Gavin, safe and soon."

Alida nodded.

She held the bag tightly in one hand, then stood on her tiptoes and rose slowly, beating her wings in a steady rhythm.

She circled the house twice, getting used to the weight of the bag.

Then she waved with her free hand and started off. She flew carefully.

It was hard to keep her balance at first, but she got better at it.

She stayed high above the ground and followed the Blue River until she got close to Ash Grove. Then she turned and stayed above the forest, flying lower, closer to the treetops.

She held the bag against her chest.

Once she was far enough away from Ash Grove, she used the road to guide her. She stayed far off to one side. She flew higher and higher. Travelers who happened to look up would see a dot in the distance. They would think she was a bird.

The earth looked strange so far below her.

The forest went on and on, in every direction, and the road looked like a single brown thread in a deep green blanket. Lord Dunraven's lands seemed endless.

By sunset Alida was tired.

She found a stand of willow trees near a creek, far from the road.

She didn't know how to make a proper faerie's nest, but the highest willow branches were slender and easy to weave into a sturdy tangle. She wrapped up in her blanket and stared at the darkening sky. And so she fell asleep beneath the moon, far above the ground, swaying with a whispering breeze.

When she woke, there were still stars overhead. She stretched and drank from the bottle of rainwater. She was hungry, too. She ate six of Ruth's delicious roses. They were sweet and tender and wonderful, and she ate them slowly, waiting for dawn.

When it was light enough to fly, she spread her wings and flew again.

She was careful not to come too close to the town at the bottom of the hill. Some people were already awake. There were lit lamps in a few of the windows.

Just as the sun came up, Alida spotted the

wide clearing in the forest that surrounded Lord Dunraven's castle.

It was even bigger than she had thought the night she and Gavin had escaped.

The ground floor was wider than any of the others, but even the dark stone towers were massive. They were beautiful in the dawn light.

Alida flew in a low, wide circle and found a rocky ridge.

She set her bag on top of a stone shaped like a giant's tooth.

Then she stared at the castle.

She didn't want to go inside it.

The corridors were like a maze.

But how else could she get Gavin out? Even if she somehow broke a window, how could he get down off the castle roof? She was afraid to try to carry him.

She wasn't at all sure her wings would be strong enough to keep them both in the air.

Alida stared at the jumble of stones on the ridge. She had suddenly been able to fly when Kip had scared her. She was certainly scared now.

Faeries could lift dogs and huge stones and many other things without touching them.

Alida found a fist-size stone and tried to make it rise into the air. She couldn't. She tried over and over. The stone didn't move at all.

Angry with herself, she rolled up her shawl and tucked it under her arm.

Then she stood on her toes.

She took a deep breath and rose into the air.

She was still afraid.

But it didn't matter.

If Gavin hadn't been brave, she would still be locked in that little chamber. She would find him. Then she would find a way to help him.

First she flew in a wide circle around the castle. She counted the towers. There weren't ten, as she had thought the night Gavin had helped her escape. There were thirteen.

Most of them had windows.

Only four of them were like the one she had been in—barred with iron.

She flew a little closer.

There were guards near the main entrances. But they were watching the road, the meadows, and the forest—not the sky.

None of them was near the barn.

Alida flew straight up, then leveled out until she was over the stables.

Coming down, she flew fast, slowing just enough to land running.

She hid behind one of the fancy carriages. Once she was sure no one had seen her, she put on her shawl to hide her wings.

She tied the ends in a careful knot.

Then she walked closer, trying to remember

where the door had been. Everything looked very different in the daylight.

Just like the castle, Lord Dunraven's barn was much bigger than she had thought.

When she finally spotted the double doors John had opened to lead the mare out, she tiptoed inside.

She could hear two men talking in low voices.

She squeezed between the wall and a stack of hay. She folded her wings tightly against her back beneath the shawl and hid, listening.

For a long time, she couldn't quite hear what they were saying.

Then they turned and walked toward her.

"How's the bay mare doing?" one of them asked the other.

"Healing fast," came the answer, and Alida sighed in relief. It was John's voice.

She waited until the second man left, then she peeked out.

John was looking at her. Somehow he had known she was there. He smiled.

"I came to find Gavin," she said.

"I knew you would," he answered. "You are like your mother. Loyal and true."

"Do you know where Gavin is?" Alida asked.

John shook his head. "But I don't think he's in any of the towers. Lord Dunraven has my stable boys run the food trays up, and there haven't been any new prisoners for a long time."

Alida's heart sank, but she nodded and thanked him. "Do you know where my family is?" she asked, then held her breath.

John shook his head sadly. "No. I miss them all." He sighed. "When you find them, please give them my best wishes."

Alida stared at him, questions rushing into her mind. But there was no time. Not now.

"I'll have the stable boys exercising horses all day long," he said. "Lots of noise and commotion."

Alida understood instantly. "Thank you."

He looked into her eyes. "It isn't my place to explain anything to you," he said. "Your mother will, when you find her. But I never meant to harm you."

There was sorrow in his eyes, and kindness. "I believe you," she told him.

He smiled. "If you need my help, I will be in the stables," he said, and walked away.

Chapter

10

John kept his word.

It wasn't long before ten stable boys—each of them riding one horse and leading three—were galloping in long circles around the castle.

The guards posted outside every door were watching the horses pounding past them.

Thanks to John's cleverness, they would be less likely to hear any sounds she made or to look *up*.

Alida started with the towers, just to make sure.

She landed lightly beside each window and peeked in.

The first one was empty, then the next, and the next, and the next.

At the fifth one, she noticed the crack in the stone.

She hovered, then turned in the air and looked down.

She recognized the shapes of the trees, the angle of the road.

This was her tower—this was the little room she had lived in for so long.

She went back to the window and looked inside. Gavin was not in the chamber. No one was. Alida stared at the bed, the stone floor.

If the guards caught her, Lord Dunraven would lock her in the chamber again.

She never wanted to be alone ever again, waiting, listening for footsteps. The thought made her tremble.

Fighting her fear, Alida flew on. John had been right. All the tower rooms were empty.

Working her way downward, looking into every window, she flew close to the stone walls. She was

careful not to make a sound, even though the horses were galloping below.

Every window was interesting.

She saw empty ballrooms. The floors were polished stone. There were mirrors framed in gold.

She saw women cleaning a huge chamber with rows of wide wooden tables.

The next room was stacked with coiled rope. Men were hunched over long tables, braiding long, dried grass together.

Alida flitted past before anyone looked up.

Looking into the next window, she saw glass tables and velvet chairs, arranged on a deep blue carpet. She kept going. Some of the bedchambers were twice as big as Ruth's whole house.

The kitchen had a hearth big enough to roast a whole cow. The windows were open. The smell of wood smoke, bread, meat, and onions drifted out.

Alida glided past, quick and unseen.

By the time she got to the lowest floor, she was starting to worry. What if she *couldn't* find Gavin this way? What would she do?

She hovered, listening to the sound of the horses galloping in the clearing below, trying to think.

The ground floor was much taller and wider than any of the others—it was the strong, solid base of the castle.

But it had no windows at all. How would she ever find him?

Alida landed and knelt, staying out of sight, trying to decide what to do.

She remembered the barred doors she had seen when she and Gavin had walked the long passages on their way out.

The rooms had high ceilings, but if there were no windows, how were they lit?

With lamps and lanterns?

The air would be thick with smoke unless there were windows or chimneys to carry it outside. She noticed narrow, wooden, peaked roofs here and there.

She went to look.

Beneath each little roof, there was a long, narrow gap in the stone.

No glass.

No iron bars.

Just an opening made to let in as much fresh air as possible. The little roofs were to keep out the rain.

Alida crouched beside the first one, ducking under the roof to peek into the huge room.

Far below her, men stood leaning against the walls, talking in low voices.

She jerked back when one of them shouted. She was sure he had spotted her.

But then someone else yelled.

They were arguing. The stone ceiling was so high that their voices echoed.

Alida caught her breath, almost sure this was one

of the barred rooms she and Gavin had passed.

She looked again, squinting to see better, then leaned back.

The men were all wearing torn shirts and tattered trousers.

They weren't guards. They were prisoners.

Peering down, she looked at each man in the vast chamber below her, one by one.

Gavin wasn't among them.

She flew to the next little roof. The room was even bigger. There were many prisoners, but Gavin wasn't there, either.

The next room was smaller. There was only one prisoner inside it. She recognized him instantly.

Gavin was walking in a slow circle, round and round. Alida slid through the slit in the stone and glided to the floor.

He whirled around, startled.

When he recognized her, he smiled. "You can fly now!"

Alida nodded. Whispering, she told him his grandmother was well.

His eyes lit up. "She is? Did you—"

"Ruth had already cured her," Alida said. Then she explained how Kip had taught her to fly, and Gavin laughed a little. She was about to admit that she had lied, but he leaned closer to whisper.

"Someone saw us leave," he told her. "But in the dark, they couldn't see that there were two riders, not one." He paused and listened, glancing at the door, before he went on. "The guards found the bracelet. So I am a thief. I will be put to hard labor for a year, but no one knows you're gone."

He stopped again, listening.

When he was sure no one was coming, he smiled. "Thank you so much for coming to say good-bye, to tell me about my grandmother. I was so worried."

Alida shook her head. "I didn't come to say good-bye," she told him. "I came to help you the way you helped me."

He pointed up at the gap in the stone, far overhead. "But I can't fly, Alida."

She nodded, then told him how faeires could make things float in the air. "I tried this morning and couldn't do it," she said, "but I will keep practicing, and I will come back and—"

The sound of heavy footsteps in the corridor made them both glance at the door.

He took her hand. "They could be coming to get me. You need to go now."

Alida hesitated. The footsteps got louder. "Where will they take you?"

He shrugged. "Probably one of Lord Dunraven's silver mines."

Alida could hear the dread in his voice. "I will follow you if they—"

"No!" Gavin whispered. "The mines are dangerous. Hurry, before they open the door!"

Alida flew upward, sliding back through the long, narrow opening in the stone. But she didn't fly away. Hidden by the little roof, she watched.

Gavin was standing very still, facing the door.

His feet were spread wide, like he was bracing himself.

All of this was so wrong, so unfair. He had just wanted to save his grandmother. He was kind. And he wasn't a thief. He had just pretended to be one to protect her.

Alida could hear the sound of heavy boots on the stone, coming closer. There had to be something she could do to help him. There *had* to be.

And, just like she had suddenly known how to fly, Alida suddenly knew how to lift him.

She took a long breath while she let the magic weave itself inside her heart.

The footsteps were getting louder.

Alida knew she had to hurry.

She stared at Gavin's cot and lifted it a handsbreadth off the floor.

Could she do this? She narrowed her eyes and let the magic begin to work.

Gavin was facing away from her when his feet left the ground.

He flailed his arms, and then arched backward to look up at the ceiling. Alida could tell the instant he spotted her. He lowered his arms and closed his eyes.

He was trying not to make it harder, trying to trust her.

Alida lifted him higher, and higher and higher.

And that part was easy.

Fitting him through the narrow gap in the stone was going to be much harder.

She heard the footsteps stop outside the door.

"Keep your eyes closed," she whispered. "Don't make a sound."

She saw him nod. Then the chamber door banged open, far, far below. She steadied herself and concentrated.

"Hiding won't keep you out of the mines, thief!" one of the guards shouted. "I have no time for children's games."

Gavin held completely still.

Alida held tight to the magic inside herself.

None of the guards looked up.

There was a silence, then another man spoke. "Maybe he's gone."

"Where?" the first guard demanded. There was no answer. "Turn the bed over! Go through the blankets! He has to be here!"

"I am going to move you a little," Alida breathed.

Gavin nodded without opening his eyes.

While the guards ran to Gavin's cot and shook out the blankets, she concentrated, reweaving the magic, so that Gavin floated along slowly, away from the gap in the stone, away from the little bit of daylight that found its way inside.

By the time the guards decided to glance upward

at the high stone ceiling, they could not see Gavin in the shadows.

"Check the corridor!" the first guard shouted suddenly. "He must have slipped out after we walked in!"

They ran out, slamming the door closed behind them.

In the silence, Alida could hear Gavin breathing. She sat back, measuring the gap in the stone. If he stretched out, his hands over his head . . .

"They will be back soon," he whispered.

"I think I can get you out," she whispered back.

There was a long silence. Then he whispered three words.

"I trust you."

Alida slowly moved Gavin toward her.

She could feel her own heart beating, but she could also feel the magic working, steady and strong.

When he was close enough, she explained what he had to do. "Move slowly and carefully. Straighten out. Put your hands above your head like you are stretching."

Without opening his eyes, Gavin did it.

Alida moved him again, lining him up with the gap in the stone.

Once he was positioned perfectly, she leaned forward.

"Hold still," she reminded him. Then she lifted him straight up. His right shoulder bumped the stone, but he stayed still. Alida lifted him a little farther, then moved him to the side.

"Even once you feel the roof beneath you," she said as she set him down, "don't move before you look. You could fall back in."

Gavin opened his eyes and lifted his head, just enough to see. Then he eased his way out from beneath the little roof.

Alida ducked out after him.

Gavin was standing up, looking at the forest, his eyes wide.

"Crouch," she said. "Just in case a guard looks up."

He sat down. "Magic," he said softly, "is real."

She nodded and smiled.

Then they both laughed—very quietly.

Chapter

11

Standing on the ridge, on top of the giant's-tooth rock, Alida and Gavin could see the castle. They watched the guards gallop off down the road.

That evening they saw the guards come back, and Alida knew it was safe to travel.

Lord Dunraven had given up the search, at least for now.

John was happy to see them both when they came late that night to say good-bye. He gave Gavin a sack of fresh bread and loaned him the white mare again.

They waited for the moon to set.

Then Alida flew around the castle, listening. Besides the usual guards, no one was outside.

They led the mare quietly into the woods, and this time no one saw them leave.

All the way to Ash Grove, they hid in the daytime and traveled only at night.

Now and then Alida would spread her wings and fly straight up, to look around, to make sure no guards were on the road behind them.

When they got to Ruth's house, Molly was so happy she cried. She cooked an herbed stew for the humans. Ruth picked a dozen fresh roses and some sweet phlox for Alida.

"What will you do now?" Ruth asked while they ate supper. "You are welcome here, both of you."

Alida thanked her. "But I can't stay. I don't want to bring trouble to the kindest people I know. And I really want to find my family."

"The queen will be uneasy about all this," Molly said quietly. "You must be careful."

"The queen?" Alida asked.

"Your mother," said Ruth. "She's the queen of the faeries."

Alida blinked. "*My* mother is a queen?"

Molly nodded. "She must be. You know that all the stories say old Lord Dunraven forced the faeries, the unicorns, and the dragons out of his lands forever?"

Alida nodded, imagining how scared her family must have been.

"The guards rode through the forests day and night," Molly told her. "They hunted the unicorns with arrows and spears and they harried the dragons in their cliffs so they couldn't hatch eggs and raise their young. But the faeries made a promise."

Alida stared at Molly, already knowing what she was going to say.

"They gave up a faerie princess, to be kept safe in Dunraven's castle. But she would only be safe if the faeries went away, and never spoke to another human being."

Ruth was nodding. "No human has had a friend among the magic folk since then."

"Except my grandson," Molly whispered.

Alida glanced at Gavin. "Will you come with me to find my family?" she asked him.

He glanced at his grandmother. She nodded. "Yes, Princess Alida," he said.

Alida made a face at him—and they all laughed.

As they cleaned up the kitchen, Gavin asked Ruth to return the white mare to John. She promised she would. And then there was nothing more to say.

Alida lay awake a long time before she slept.

Even so, she woke at dawn, scared and excited.

Everyone cried a little, hugging, saying good-bye. Then they just looked at one another without speaking for a moment.

Alida faced Gavin. "Are you ready?"

He nodded.

She pulled the feather-light shawl over her wings.

Then they started off, walking side by side away from Ash Grove—toward the wild lands.

Read on for more

The Faeries' Promise

FOLLOWING MAGIC, Book 2
in the Faeries' Promise series

The sun was rising.

It would be a warm, fine day.

Alida turned back to wave good-bye to Ruth Oakes and Gavin's grandmother.

They smiled at her, but Alida could tell they were worried. She was a little scared. She didn't want to leave Ruth's wonderful house near the town of Ash Grove. But she had no choice.

She glanced at Gavin.

He looked a little nervous too.

Alida was so grateful that he was coming with her.

They stopped at the edge of the woods and both waved one last time.

Then they walked into the trees.

The grayish light of dawn was even dimmer beneath the old oaks. The trees smelled like home to Alida. That made her so happy—and so sad—that she stopped and closed her eyes, breathing deeply.

When she opened them, Gavin was looking at her. "Do you know which way we should go?"

Alida shook her head. Gavin had thought Ruth might know where the faeries had gone when old Lord Dunraven made his law, but she didn't. No one did.

"We have to find the meadow I remember," Alida said. "I'm hoping my mother left something there for me."

Gavin lifted his eyebrows, but he didn't ask questions, and she was glad. She wasn't at all sure they would find anything in the meadow, and she had no idea what she would do if they didn't.

"Will you recognize the right place?" Gavin asked.

"Yes," Alida said. She was sure of that, even though she hadn't seen it in a long, long time. She remembered her family's home very clearly.

There was a noisy stream that ran across one end of the meadow.

At the other end there was a huge egg-shaped rock.

And there were many old oak trees, perfect for faerie nests. Everyone had slept in the treetops. She and her older sister had snuggled together if the night was chilly. Terra had been patient with her, holding her hand when there was no moon and she was afraid of the dark. Terra was the eldest, so when their mother got old, she would become queen. Alida knew she would be kind and fair, like their mother.

Alida sighed. She missed her family so much. "I hope it isn't too far from Ash Grove," she said, and turned to look at Gavin.

He nodded. "We'll just keep looking until we find it."

Alida smiled at him.

They had both brought rolled-up blankets to keep them warm at night.

Alida's was magical—her mother had woven it before she was born.

Gavin's was warm and soft, a gift from his grandmother. And he had a flint and striker in his pocket in case they needed to make a fire.

He was carrying a cloth sack full of bread and cheese too.

Alida didn't have to bring anything to eat; she would be able to find proper faerie food—there were spring flowers everywhere.

Walking through the oak trees, Alida was very happy. The air was perfumed with dew and sunshine and spring. It was as beautiful as she remembered.

She was so excited.

She couldn't wait to find the meadow.

Many faerie families had lived there when she was little.

All the faerie children had played games and were taught magic. Alida had just begun to learn when Lord Dunraven took her away.

Alida sighed, remembering the faerie lights, the stars, and how the stream had chuckled and whispered. Oh, how she had missed that sound. Oh, how she longed to see her family. She had taught herself to fly, and she knew they would be proud of her.

But of course they wouldn't be living in the meadow anymore.

Old Lord Dunraven's law had changed every-thing.

Alida walked a little faster, staying ahead of Gavin.

She didn't want him to see how sad it made her to think about her home being empty. Once she had blinked away the tears, she glanced back at him.

"I wish Ruth Oakes and your grandmother had known where my family ended up."

"I think it was probably part of the faeries' promise not to tell humans where they were going," Gavin said.

Alida slowed until they were walking side by side. "Did your grandmother tell you that? Was it in the old stories?"

Gavin shook his head. "But it makes sense. If old Lord Dunraven wanted to keep people and faeries from being friends, he wouldn't want them living close."

"And to make the faeries keep their promise, he took me away," Alida said quietly.

Gavin nodded. "It must have been a terrible decision for your family."

Alida felt a stirring in her heart.

Locked in the tower in Lord Dunraven's castle, she had often wondered why her parents never came to help her. But now she knew why. They had been forced to make a promise to old Lord Dunraven.

Alida glanced up at the trees.

Her mother had known that Lord Dunraven would not hurt her as long as the faeries kept their promise to stay away from humans.

And he hadn't.

No one had said a single harsh word to her.

But she had been locked in a stone tower.

It had been so lonely.

"Don't worry," Gavin said.

She glanced at him. "Do I look worried?"

He nodded. "But John will keep his word. Lord Dunraven won't have any reason to suspect you are gone."

Alida knew he was right.

But she had to be careful.

She could never be sure when they might come upon a human being.

And if anyone realized she was a faerie, not just a small girl, people would talk.

The news would spread.

And then Lord Dunraven's guards *would* come looking for her.

"Alida?"

She turned; Gavin was pointing at a narrow road that ran between the trees. Without saying a word, they both veered away from it.

And as they walked, Alida pulled her shawl higher, making sure it covered her wings.